Susan Salidor

I'VE GOT PEACE
IN MY FINGERS

This book is dedicated to my family:
Jay Rehak (first and last), Hope and
Hannah Rehak and Ali Malik.
Without you, there would be little peace,
fewer kind words and much less love in my life.

Thanks also to my friend Susan Klein
and to my illustrator, Natalka Soiko,
whose artwork and patience
have made a dream come true.

Susan Salidor

 Sideline Ink Publishing

No part of this book may be reproduced in whole or in part, without the expressed written consent of the publisher.

For information regarding permission, please write to Sideline Ink Publishing, Chicago IL 60625.

ISBN: 978-0-9992905-9-0
Ingram Spark Edition

This book belongs to

· ·

who has the power
to be
a peacemaker,
to use
kind words, and
to be loving
and loved
in return.

I'VE GOT PEACE, PEACE, PEACE IN MY FINGERS

WATCH WHAT I CAN DO.

I'VE GOT PEACE, PEACE, PEACE IN MY FINGERS

WORDS, WORDS, WORDS
IN MY HEAD...

I've Got Peace In My Fingers

Susan Salidor
transcribed by Ted Hearne

Slow Shuffle

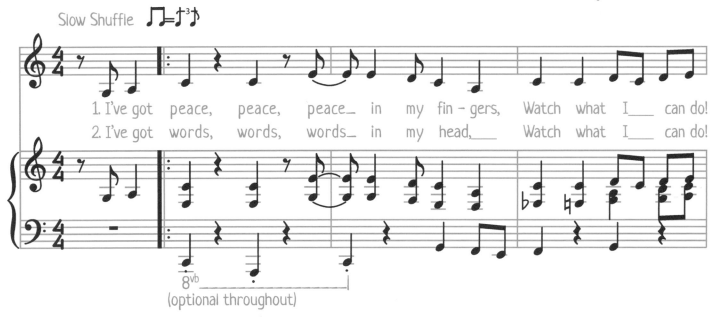

1. I've got peace, peace, peace___ in my fin - gers, Watch what I___ can do!
2. I've got words, words, words___ in my head,___ Watch what I___ can do!

8vb
(optional throughout)

I've got peace, peace, peace___ in my fin-gers, I'm gon-na shake hands with you!
I've got words, words, words___ in my head,___ I'm gon-na talk things ov-er with you!

3. I've got love, love, love in my heart
   Watch what I can do!
   I've got love, love, love in my heart
   I'm gonna give some to you!